LITTLE FOX

LITTLE FOX

by MARILYN JANOVITZ

North-South Books · New York · London

Little Fox liked to climb. Not on his chair, it was too small.
And Father's chair was too big. But Mother's chair was just right.
"That chair is not for climbing," said Mother.

Little Fox liked to jump. Not on his chair, it was too soft.
And Father's chair was too hard. But Mother's chair was just right.
"That chair is not for jumping," said Mother.

Mother's chair was just right for riding, too.
On it he won every race.
"That chair is going to break!" warned Mother.

And one day, as Little Fox lay in the chair sleeping . . .

that's exactly what happened.
"Oh, dear!" cried Mother.
"Oh, my!" cried Father.

"I didn't mean to break it," said Little Fox sadly.
Father picked up the pieces and put them in back,
with the other broken things.

"Where am I going to sit now?" asked Mother.

"You can sit in my chair," said Little Fox.
 So Mother Fox did.
"This chair is not right," she said. "It is too small and too soft."

"Try my chair," said Father Fox.

So Mother Fox did.

"This chair is not right," she said. "It is too big and too hard."

"Well then," said Father Fox, "we will buy you a new chair."

The next day, Father Fox, Mother Fox, and Little Fox went to the chair store.

"Let's get this one," called Little Fox.

"Oh, no," said Mother. "That's not the right chair for me."

"Look," said Father. "This chair can do everything!"

"I don't need a chair that can do everything," said Mother.
"But perhaps I'll try some of the others."

And that's just what Mother Fox did.
She sat in one chair, and then she sat in another.

Then she sat in the next one and then the one after that
until she had tried each and every chair in the entire store.

"Let's go home," said Mother. "Not one of these chairs is the right chair for me."

The next day, Little Fox sat in his small, soft chair and Father Fox sat in his big, hard chair. In between was an empty space where Mother's chair had been.

Little Fox whispered to Father, and off they went, into the back.

They measured, they sawed, they hammered, they glued, and before long Mother's chair was back together again.

They placed it carefully in the empty space in between.
"We have one more chair for you to try!" called Little Fox.

"Well, let's see," said Mother as she sat down. "Oh, yes," she said,
"this chair is just right."

"Little Fox," said Mother, "come and sit with me. We'll read a story."

"On your chair?" asked Little Fox.
"Why, of course," said Mother. "That's what chairs are for."

She lifted Little Fox up and they cuddled close.
"I like to read," said Little Fox.
And for reading, Mother's chair was just right.

To Estelle

Copyright © 1999 by Marilyn Janovitz

Published in the United States by North-South Books Inc., New York.
Published simultaneously in Great Britain, Canada, Australia, and New Zealand in 1999
by North-South Books, an imprint of Nord-Süd Verlag AG, Gossau Zürich, Switzerland.

Library of Congress Cataloging-in-Publication Data is available.
A CIP catalogue record for this book is available from The British Library.

The illustrations in this book were created
with colored pencil and watercolor.
Designed by Marc Cheshire

ISBN 0-7358-1160-1 (trade binding)
1 3 5 7 9 TB 10 8 6 4 2
ISBN 0-7358-1161-X (library binding)
1 3 5 7 9 LB 10 8 6 4 2
Printed in Belgium